THIS IS NOT A
POEM/STORY

© 2023 Randolph Walker, Jr.
All rights reserved.
Cover image used courtesy of Joshua Oyebanji

ISBN: 9781020001376 (Paperback)
ISBN: 9781020001406 (Ebook)

Library of Congress Control Number: 2023906456

First Edition

10 9 8 7 6 5 4 3 2

Black and Square
Hampton Roads, VA

THIS IS NOT A POEM/STORY

100-WORD STORIES

RAN WALKER

CONTENTS

PART 2

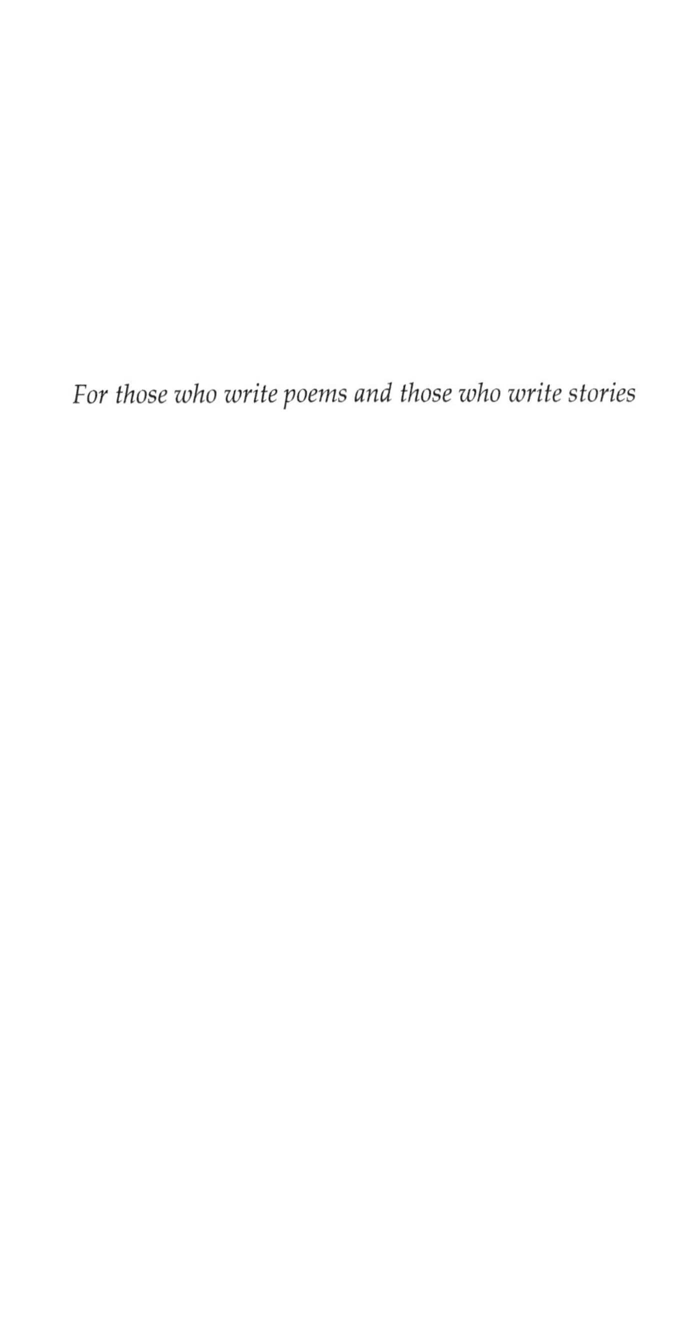

For those who write poems and those who write stories

Over these past couple of years, the 100-word story has provided me with an amazing canvas on which to try some radically creative ideas. The book you hold in your hands is a byproduct of several different ideas I've been considering over this past year, the first of which is this: what differentiates microfiction from a prose poem?

Like other microfictionists who have come before me, I see the line as being extremely fine, so much so that I decided to write a book that contained both microfiction and poetry.

I have divided the book into sections (Part 1: This Is Not a Poem and Part 2: This Is Not a Story), but many readers are likely to think that there is very little difference in the two forms (at least the way I write them). And that, I feel, is the point. A narrative prose poem and a poetic microfiction story can be nearly identical. Rather than wrestle to label these pieces, though, I would recommend you simply enjoy them.

The second issue I've been considering more

deeply is how Afrosurrealism can be translated into microfiction in a meaningful way. In that regard, I have drawn inspiration from Henry Dumas, Donald Glover, Thylias Moss, Toni Morrison, Jordan Peele, Ishmael Reed, Gloria Naylor, Victor LaValle, Tananarive Due, Thundercat, Kendrick Lamar, and a host of other Black creators who have navigated this space.

I have also drawn inspiration from Amiri Baraka's, D. Scot Miller's, and Rochelle Spencer's work in the area of Afrosurrealism. While many of these pieces tap into Afrosurrealism, I have also included stories that may be more aptly described as Afrofuturistic and Afro Gothic, as well.

In my short story collection *Portable Black Magic: Tales of the Afro Strange*, I explored the space of Afro speculative fiction, but having now found a true passion for microfiction, I have committed myself to exploring these ideas in a much smaller, more compact space.

As you explore these tiny works, I hope you will enjoy them for their own sake—but for those of you who like Easter eggs, there are definitely a few sprinkled throughout this book.

I hope you enjoy this labor of love.

Onward and upward (and even sideways),

Ran Walker

THIS IS NOT A POEM/STORY

Exit, pursued by a bear.

WILLIAM SHAKESPEARE

PART 1

THIS IS NOT A POEM

THIS IS NOT A POEM

THIS IS NOT A POEM. It's a story.

In this story a boy writes a poem, watching the words crawl slowly from his pencil, the graphite pulling itself like that character in the movie who's dragging his leg, telling the others, "Leave me behind. Save yourselves!"

The words are forming images in his mind, images he hopes will bring her the comfort she so desperately seeks.

His grandmother had become an angel, too, and someone had written a poem for him.

It was amazing, the comforting power of words.

So he's writing this poem for her, but also for himself.

2

———————————

THE NOVELIST

ONE DAY he will get an idea for a book. He will write it, and it will come out like drivel. Then he will write it again, and it will get only slightly better. He will abandon this idea. Later, he will read a book and remember his old idea. He will look at the second draft and realize it wasn't completely irredeemable. He will write a new draft. It will get better, even though it will never look exactly like he originally envisioned it. He will learn to love this new book, and one day it will get published.

BLANKETS

IT WAS ONLY after he left that she realized the old blanket had been too small. She coiled her five-foot frame on the couch, like a boa constrictor resisting brumation, hoping to squeeze the last bit of warmth out of the covering, its length just short enough that the winter air found the thin space between her pajamas and socks, reminding her he was no longer there to block out the cold. She considered calling him to come over—to come home—but he had made his choice. And so had she.

She would buy a new blanket tomorrow morning.

BOJOULÉ WILLIAMS THREATENS TO COME OUT OF RETIREMENT

DEAR GENERAL MANAGER of [unnamed NFL team]:

I realize that your team has had some issues on offense lately, largely due to the underwhelming performance of your wide receiver corps. To that end, I wanted to inform you that I'm coming out of retirement, after having played slot in Pee Wee league, and am currently available.

I can drop passes, fumble the ball, mess up routes, give up on plays, and not find the ball for a fraction of what you're paying now.

Get at me. I'll be here on my recliner.

Take care, and go [team nickname]!

Bojoulé Williams

I FEEL STUPID AND CONTAGIOUS

THE KIDS at school referred to her as the girl who lived in the haunted house. They eyed her curiously, observing how she ate her lunch, how she dressed, even how she held her pencil, always afraid to make fun of her for fear that she'd send a haint or a poltergeist to their homes and turn them into someone…like her.

She wished her father had never told the news reporter any of that, that some things should remain private, including whether or not her ancestors ever chose to leave the house at the end of Magnolia Terrace Lane.

6

SOPORIFIC

THE BEDPOSTS WERE MADE of stacked books, as were the mattress and pillows, though they were covered in papyrus inscribed with the works of her favorite poets, and she slept peacefully each night, in spite of the firmness of the bed, her mind racing with stories that seemed to seep into the pores of her skin from every angle, osmotic entertainment that edified her insatiable love of literature.

Many of the books she had never read, but she felt as if she had, having been so close to them for so long, those arcane pages endlessly wooing her to sleep.

STRAYS

"Can I keep it?" Stephanie said, jumping up and down, tugging on her mother's dress.

"Keep what?"

"That!" Stephanie pointed at the massive, hairy beast in the yard.

The beast's hair was long, concealing its muscular frame, but its enormity was still evident, as it sat on its haunches, its clawed hands resting in the grass.

"Please!" Stephanie added excitedly.

Her mother stared at the beast and shook her head.

"Where would we put it?" her mother finally responded. "We don't have the space to keep every beast you bring home."

So Stephanie reluctantly stepped outside and shooed it away.

RAINBOW

WHEN TONY PROMISED he'd bring a rainbow to school on Friday, no one believed him—except Alisha, who was known to believe in such things.

When Friday came, nearly everyone in the schoolyard gathered around him during recess, their collective curiosity as thick as a malt milkshake, all of them watching his clasped hands.

"Stand back," Tony said, turning his face away in anticipation.

His hands shot open and seven colors leaped from his palms in an august arch.

The kids, nearly blinded, gasped in astonishment, but only Alisha stood there, smiling, her sunglasses having already been put in place.

JESS AND TOBIN DECIDE TO MAKE A FILM

"I HATE horror movies where everybody gets killed. I mean, what's the point?"

"I guess they need to set up the killer for the sequel."

"But can't they at least have one of those—what do you call them—uh, *final girls*?"

"It seems like they would. Personally, I feel there is value in following the tropes of the genre."

"Who are you telling?!"

"Maybe we should make our own horror film."

"Well, at least we could have a final girl, someone to battle the killer and believe that she's killed him."

"But he'll be back."

"Of course he will."

THE STRANGER IN SEAT 32B

SHE REFUSED to let him sleep.

Flying made her nervous, she said, and to calm her nerves, she talked incessantly. He, too, was a nervous flyer, which is why he preferred to be unconscious throughout the flight, but she would't allow him the peace of his dreams.

He accepted the fact that if the plane went down, he'd be wide awake. He knew she'd scream and carry on something awful (she was definitely the type). If he couldn't die in peace, though, maybe he'd scream along with her, even make a contest of it, have one last bit of fun.

PURA VIDA

WE BARREL DOWN THE ZIP-LINE, thousands of rainforest canopies covering our shadows, our feet dangling, hearts racing, eyes barely able to make out the red, blue, and yellow of macaws or the yellow and black of the toucans. The azure sky waves at us, the green beneath us bowing beneath our Nikes as if we are some kind of royalty. But we are just plebeians in this Eden, specks of dust in the hands of the Almighty, passing through, our detour one that celebrates life, like the Christmas gift we swore we'd never get, but that our parents tucked away.

WILL SOMEBODY WEAR ME TO THE FAIR?

FOR MINNIE RIPERTON

I SEE HER APPROACHING, her beautiful, broad smile radiating energy, the sun kissing her gently upon her forehead, a sweet hum emanating from behind her lips, like a jewel safely ensconced in the belly of an old oak treasure chest lined in velvet. She is coming for me, and I want to go with her.

When she reaches for me, I surrender to her touch.

"Voulez-vous venir avec moi?" she whispers softly, gently plucking me, as if I were the string of a forlorn guitar.

She will tuck me behind her ear, my petals a satellite of her afro.

AN INTRODUCTION

VALERIE WONDERS what could have been had she not introduced him to her best friend. Now she watches their kids play on a jungle gym in their backyard, the tiny playhouse a near replica of the mansion that rests in front of it, the German and Italian cars in the garage, and the way he rests his hand gently around her waist, her snuggling against him, body aglow.

Valerie wonders if this could have been *her* life, or if she was always destined to be the godmother, the "play" auntie, the lonely friend who visits, always bearing the largest grin.

HOLDEN

It's not my fault.

He wasn't a real hunter anyway.

Phony people take you out into the middle of the woods, claiming to be expert marksmen, with these vests, these hats, placing the steel in my hands to scope and shoot the animal in front of me, but all of these things look the same.

How is orange for safety if you can't make out orange from brown from green from red[1]?

If you hide in and around trees, how do I know what to shoot?

It's not my fault.

And this hat—is it orange, brown, green, or *red*?

---

1. According to research done by San Francisco State University, 5% of females and 8% of males have some form of colorblindness.

THE HAUNTING

THE RUMBLINGS of a ghost haunting the library emerged roughly four years after the suicide, just enough time for those who knew the true story to have graduated and moved on, leaving behind a clueless student body with only rumors to spark their restless imaginations. He was said to walk the seventh floor in the late evening, this story now so prevalent that even the security guards drew straws to see who would venture up there to secure the floor for closing.

There were no reliable accounts of a sighting, but it didn't matter. When something is haunted, it's haunted.

PURPLE

HE WOULD LATER ADMIT he'd fallen for her the moment he first saw her standing in front of Frank's Hardware in her white pedal pushers, purple popsicle in hand. He'd nearly dropped the slingshot he'd wrestled together from a small tree branch and thick rubber band.

It'd taken two summers of passing messages back and forth between friends until he felt comfortable enough to pass her a note asking if she'd be his girl.

It was the one story he continued to tell people, even as a widower some years later, always wondering how good that popsicle must have tasted.

BARACK IS MY FRIEND

EVERY NOW AND then I dream about Barack Obama.

In my dreams we're friends, even though he can barely remember me from the conversations I've had with him in my other dreams.

Still, we hit it off famously and end up waxing poetic on nearly everything.

I think, *No one will ever believe I am friends with Barack,* so I take out my phone. I wrestle with it, trying to open the camera app, but it never works —because, in dreams, the user interface is always confusing.

I wake, never having gotten the picture, but still optimistic about next time.

ON LOVE AND FARTING

During the first time I met her family, her little brother ran into the den and farted, then ran away. Her father began laughing. My then-girlfriend joined in, and soon I, too, was laughing.

Every once in a while, during a visit, the brother would do the same thing or her dad would hike up his leg and let loose, his laughter causing his flatulence to start and stop. Everyone would laugh, including my now-fiancee.

One night in bed, shortly after we'd married, I farted, expecting her to laugh. Instead, she responded, "I thought I'd finally gotten away from that."

19
____

JUST DO IT

Every Saturday, like clockwork, she exits her apartment at 7 AM and trots in place for a few minutes, then stretches, her toned brown legs peeking out from her running shorts, her volt-colored Air Maxes matching only her spirit. I stand in the window of my apartment, a mug of coffee in my hand, and wave to her. She waves back, her smile lingering long after she's started her run. I've considered walking over and speaking to her, but my nerves get the better of me and I give up, only to wake early the following Saturday and try again.

20

———————

THE PARAMOUR

His indefatigability in the bedroom was a thing of legend, his refractory period the length of a rocket's countdown to blast off—if that. Though quantity mattered in some respects, his reputation had been carefully and diligently built upon the *quality* of his performance. It was a skill that accounted for both practice and natural ability, although he didn't flaunt it. Only his lovers knew of his prowess, which for better or worse served as a standard they tried unsuccessfully to measure their husbands against. He would always be that one who understood them in ways no one else could.

PASSE-PARTOUT

ALEX WILL NOT ADMIT this to anyone—not even herself. There is a reason she is alone (not to be confused with being lonely), and she has made a sort of peace with that.

The heart knows what it needs to be happy and complete, and Alex knows that satiation can come from only one person, but what if that person is no longer available?

She realizes she could move on, but she also knows the door would never be locked. Megan could come back to Alex one day, using the key only she possesses, and change the world, again.

WAIST DEEP

Always immaculately dressed, Terrance was often the focus of his co-workers' small talk before he logged on. Not that Terrance wasn't stylish back in the office, but since the pandemic kept them home, he'd become a sartorial wizard.

At first their compliments were playful. "Nice tie and blazer." "French cuffs?"

Then they became more animated. "Mr. Debonair!" "You're cleaner than the Board of Health!"

All of it crashed to a halt one day when Terrance stood and accidentally revealed his basketball shorts.

They were floored by this illusion, and the mundanity of the meetings quickly resumed its rightful place.

BENEATH THE PECAN TREE

THEY LAY in the shade of the pecan tree, their bellies full of drupes, a little grit still sticking to their gums.

"When I grow up, I'm moving to the city," the boy said, his hand behind his head, cushioning it from the bark.

"I think I'm going to stay here. The city is too fast for me. I just want to have a nice quiet life," she responded, twisting one of her braids.

Neither would ever bring up the topic again, but in that moment, they had realized their futures would not include the other, something they'd reluctantly accepted.

ALL IN A NAME

Eric once dated a girl named Courtney Roach. She preferred to be called "Coco."

He wondered if she'd had to deal with people making fun of her name—*he couldn't bring himself to say her first and last name together*—or if she'd been judged in the manner he was now trying desperately to avoid.

He wanted so much to look past it, to be better than that, to not dwell on the fact that she came from a family of Roaches, so it came as quite a surprise when she told him she couldn't get over *his* surname: Beverly.

CONTRITION FOR A CONTRACTION

HE'D SPENT an hour combing Hallmark for the perfect card, one that encapsulated all the emotions he had for her, the things he'd been unable to articulate in words when she was around. It was so perfect he didn't have to inscribe it, only sign it.

As she read it, though, her face gradually soured. *Had he offended her?*

Finally, he broke down and asked what was wrong.

"There's a typo here," she responded. "It says 'it's' and it should say 'its,' without the apostrophe."

He'd never considered the possessive—or that an apostrophe could, like those letters, divide them.

THE WAR OVER MY BROTHER

People thought Mama was crazy when a few folks saw her arguing with God in front of our house last summer. Unbeknownst to those nosy bystanders, she'd been going at it with Him for some time now, but it was just now spilling over into the street.

It all had to do with my brother bangin[1]—and since he wouldn't listen to Mama, Mama took it to a higher power. And the arguing ensued.

But it was clear to anyone who was paying attention that she was on the losing end of that one.

So we prayed for them both.

---

1. Participating in gang-related activities. Not to be confused with any form of sexual assault using similar phrasing.

MY SISTER'S PARTY

My sister begged me to smile at her euthanasia party. I had threatened not to go, hoping she'd change her mind, but Mom was going, so I had no choice.

Nine of us gathered at the house where our family spent summers before Dad died. One of her friends DJ'ed old school hip hop from his phone and we tried to dance, as if cancer had not attended the party.

We finally gave our farewells, all of us fighting to remain upbeat.

I died a thousand times that day, but my sister, a smile on her lips, died only once.

THE ATHENAEUM ON MLK AVENUE

Jericho Jackson died, leaving behind his three-level Victorian to a local non-profit that had little idea of what to do with it. Each floor was full of books, and they were arranged in such a way that they created a maze throughout the entire house. One board member referred to it as a "bibliophilic labyrinth."

A vote was eventually taken to ensure that there were no structural hazards, and once everything checked out, they decided to open the house, as is, to the young scholars of the community, creating the first building of its type in that particular neighborhood.

FLOWERS

She loved flowers, but often found she was allergic to most of them, having long ago let go of the more common genera long ago. Every person she ever dated was aware of this paradox: her waxing poetic over her love of flowers to only later pop antihistamine tablets so she could get a restful night of sleep.

In retrospect, she later realized, this matter could have been easily resolved by her dates purchasing faux bouquets, something nice with a blend of delicate fabrics and plastics, but, as her mom used to say, that would've been too much like right.

THE SOMNAMBULIST

OR HOW DAN HARTMAN TURNED WINSTON FORD INTO A FOOTNOTE

MOVING SIDEWALKS. Stony Jackson sliding across the stage, a soulful lyric, wet like a jheri curl, Winston Ford's voice, like thunder, reverberating through movie speakers, and blue suits in lockstep, one groove, blacker than the ink on this page. This version is the one I know, the one in my dreams.

A white man walks into a room and when he leaves, he is now the face of this song, this group, this groove—and my ten-year-old self is confused, wondering what happened and why my friends seem to believe these Black men are lip syncing a white man's voice.

THE VIEW FROM HERE

DUSK WEARS MANY COLORS: violet, magenta, cyan, navy, orange, and even midnight. Above this blanket, stars settle like diamonds spread across a picnic blanket. Anita has no desire to be any closer to heaven than she already is. She has learned that sometimes the closer you get to something, the less impressive it is. She doesn't want to know the trick of it all, where the rabbit rests, awaiting the magician to lift it by its ears from a top hat. She plants her feet firmly on earth, anchoring herself to the place where everything can be beautiful and surreal.

JANET BROWN'S REVIEW OF THE JUNKYARD OF ABSURDITIES FOR THE OAK BLUFF CHRONICLE

OR TELL ME HOW YOU REALLY FEEL

THE PLAY SEEMS to have no clear focus. It kind of goes on and on, like some interminable sentence that resists translation or even explanation. A fever dream of mundanity. The stage directions are unnecessarily copious, and the dialogue is little more than one disjointed monologue after the other. It tries to be clever, but in a "pop" kind of way, as if designed to be analyzed, ad nauseam, by a generation trained to overthink allusions and symbols in music videos. Even more, this play feels like it was never intended to be performed at all, just read to oneself.

33

———

BALANCE

LYLE SHAKES a mound of Morton Salt into his hand and makes a tight fist. He shakes his hand swiftly over the freshly-sliced watermelon wedge on the wooden box (the one that doubles as a table for playing bones).

When his wife serves him buttery rice sprinkled with sugar, she violently yanks him by his long, curly hair and plants a wet kiss upon his lips. He savors them both.

Everything good in his life is both sweet and salty and wet, metaphorically and literally, and he revels in creating that delicate balance in everything that exists in his world.

WATCHING THE WORLD PASS BY

HE STARES OUTSIDE THE WINDOW, watching the world move by on a conveyor belt. Occasionally a person turns to glance in his direction, before moving forward. He knows where they are going is not important because it doesn't exist to him, for those things are beyond the boundaries of his window.

A little girl holding a red balloon faces him, a small dog, nestled against her leg, wagging its tail. She waves a mittened hand, but her mouth is devoid of a smile. She is moving laterally, the conveyor belt carrying her off into an abyss outside the window frame.

THE BUBBLE

THE MAGICIAN PROMISED Noah if he stepped into the massive soapy bubble the giant ring would create that he'd be swept away to places that could only be reached in dreams. He glanced at his father, who seemed preoccupied with his girlfriend, then at his big brother who, in an effort to mirror his father, stood talking to some girl he'd just met at the Imaginarium. Noah nodded and stepped forward, a slight gust of wind brushing his back and sealing the bubble around him. He knew of no places in his dreams, but he went along for the ride.

AN ALTERCATION AT JEFFREY'S FISH & CHIPS

ALL ANY OF us knew was that the old fisherman was heated. He kept trying to explain to the manager about an agreement he and the owner had made, but the manager, thinking the old man a kook, continually brushed him off. It was difficult to enjoy our meals watching such an exchange.

Having had enough, the old fisherman left—which we thought signaled the end of the altercation. Minutes later he returned with a barrel, which he promptly emptied into the lobby, leaving the entire place covered in dead catfish.

He left us all to sort the matter ourselves.

37

THE RACE

FOR JESSE OWENS

I DIG two holes into the cinder to place my feet. My mind wants to race, but I breathe deeply to clear it.

In the next lane, I hear the horse neighing. It was meant to run—like me—but we should never have been put head-to-head.

Four months ago I won four gold medals in Berlin, but this is how I will feed myself today. I will race this animal, this beast called racism.

The starter will fire his gun right next to the horse's ear so I can get my head start. Then I will run my race.

FAITH AND FAUSTUS

The Devil arrived during the climax of Reverend Samuel's sermon on the last night of revival. The shrunken, old man walked past the ecstatic worshippers seated along the makeshift aisle beneath the tent. No one seemed to notice him, but when the reverend's eyes met those of the visitor, it was clear that not only did he recognize him, he feared him.

"It's time," The Devil said.

"But I'm preaching now. I'm saving souls. I'm doing the Lord's work!"

"Hey, a deal's a deal. It's time."

Reverent Samuels reluctantly followed, but he continued preaching to his congregation as he exited.

INCREMENTAL

Titus sensed his wife's hair was growing longer, but he couldn't be sure. He wanted to say something, but he knew how his wife could be about her hair. He didn't want to accidentally insult her or say something she might think ridiculous. He honestly could not tell. It seemed like it was longer each day. Maybe she was adding extensions or weave or maybe the natural ingredients she mixed together were helping it to grow.

It was only when he finally awakened inside the warm, thick curls of her hair that he realized he had been right all along.

THE DIVER

THE DIVER STOOD before us holding a thimble too small to fit on the pinkie of either hand. The thimble was filled with water, much less than what could swish around a small mouth after brushing.

"I will dive into this," he announced, to our astonishment. He then climbed a ladder that went up into the clouds.

He was so tiny we could not see him. If we had looked away at any point, we would have never believed him to even be there.

Seconds later, the water in the thimble moved.

We looked down to see him inside, smiling.

THE ONION

OR VERBOSITY AND THE ART OF WRITING MICROFICTION

ONCE UPON A TIME—WAIT, that's four words. Do I really want to spend four words opening up a 100-word story? Even more, do I want to spend another seventeen words explaining that fact? By now, I only have sixty words left. What kind of story can I possibly tell in so few words?

Hemingway used six. Monterroso used seven (eight when you translate it to English). And so I shall do the same—hopefully—with these remaining twenty words:

> *Having fancied herself an onion, she*
> *cried as they peeled back each of her*
> *layers to finally expose her core.*

42

———

SPLIT

Henry could hear the rip—actually everyone could hear it. For a moment there was complete silence. In that silence, he turned his back to the whiteboard and, as deftly as he could, swept a hand behind the seat of his pants, horrified to feel his cotton boxer briefs. It took a moment for him to register the laughing of his students or the fact that they'd retrieved their phones and were now recording his reaction.

"Will you be my secret, or will you be my shame?" he quietly asked.

Clearly uncomfortable, they moved on, pretending nothing had ever happened.

THE MODEL

HE SAT AS STILL as he could, eyes fixed on her. She glanced away toward the canvas, her hand moving in sweeping motions, her body oscillating naturally between these two foci, as if by instinct.

To celebrate their love, she'd asked to paint him, and he, never having been the focus of *any-one's* art, readily agreed. He tried to settle into his awkward pose, his body aching the entire time.

When she finally invited him to view her progress, he found himself completely distracted by the pentimento of an other man—an earlier lover?—taunting him from beneath the over-painting.

THE VOICE ACTOR

HE LOVED MORNINGS, when his voice was deepest. He'd contort his face to make it even lower and raspier. Then he'd enunciate each of his chosen words carefully. This is how he'd develop his voice to become a true crime podcaster.

He'd then pace the floor, imitating Keith Morrison, while saying phrases like "the thing about Pam" or "the thing about Helen and Olga," always careful to raise the pitch of his voice slightly at the beginning of the phrase before lowering it on the last word.

"They never saw the killer coming," he declared, oblivious to his own words.

45

HOT

THEY SAT at a small round table beneath the awning of the cafe, sipping their afternoon tea, when a completely nude man walked past them into the shop.

"It's getting hotter and hotter these days," Barron remarked.

"Yes, I read that the polar caps are melting," Liz responded.

"Global warming, they say."

"It's certainly hotter than last year—and the year before that."

"Maybe we'll need to walk around naked, too."

"I read that long robes are better to keep you cool."

Just then the naked man emerged, carrying a cup of tea.

"Enjoy your day," he offered.

They nodded.

THE NEXT CHAPTER

ONE DAY she will teach her last class, grade her last paper, attend her last graduation (for those who are neither family nor friends). She will initially enjoy the freedom of it all, but then she will sense that she now has a lack of purpose. She will take up hobbies, where she will meet with limited success. She will feel like a novice at everything except her former career.

Then something in her thinking will shift, and she will understand she must embrace being a student of the world once again and be okay with not knowing the answers.

EATING WORMS

WHEN ELVIN WAS LITTLE, he'd read a book about how to eat fried worms. It was one of those gross books that was designed to get little boys into the habit of reading. He'd loved those books so much that he even considered eating an earthworm himself. Thankfully, his mother caught him laying one on a piece of bread and stopped him.

Many years later, he walked into the kitchen to catch his own son laying an earthworm across a slice of bread. He started to stop him, but he decided instead to just watch, living vicariously through his son.

WHAT GRANDMA LEFT ME

ON HER DEATHBED, Grandma talked about how in the days shortly after "separate but equal" she'd had a white classmate who had professed to have the thumb of a Black man, some souvenir from a lynching years before, that he offered to show to kids for a dime during recess. She admitted that, after weeks, her curiosity got the better of her and she sneaked a peek through the crowd. It was purple and shrunken, like a pickled carrot she'd once eaten.

"I should've said something, but I didn't," she said, the terror still gripping her, transferring on to me.

STATEN ISLAND

SHE GRABBED her child's hand and tried to rush past the vagrant.

"But Mommy, he's wearing a Wu-Tang shirt," the little boy said.

The woman glanced back at the man—but only for a second. She tried to keep her pacing, but the little boy pulled himself away and began doubling back toward the man.

Seeing her little blond cherub approach the man unsettled her. She knew she wasn't supposed to be afraid of Black men. Hell, that was her husband's Wu-Tang sticker on the Tesla.

"Wu-Tang is for the children," the little boy offered.

The man nodded and smiled.

THE FUNERAL

THE TOWNSPEOPLE ARE BAFFLED by the mother's lack of emotion at the funeral, but she believes the body is not that of her son but of someone else. People deal with grief differently, this depleting pain, amorphous emptiness, but Jarod believes the mother. She is right. That is not her son.

He will do his job—because that's what he's been hired to do—but he saw the gills that rest beneath the collar of that starched white shirt. He remembers the astonished looks of his fellow morticians. This is not her son.

Her son is still out there somewhere.

PART 2

THIS IS NOT A STORY

THIS IS NOT A STORY

THIS IS NOT A STORY. It's a poem.

In this poem a girl writes a story, carefully guiding her grief into the barrel of her fountain pen so that, like the deluge of tears nearly blinding her vision, the ink flows freely, punctuating the page with the stains of her pain.

She thinks of the boy, his kindness—*his* loss— and she finds solace in this, knowing that she is not alone, that in the world's bountiful garden of people, there are some who shine the light of empathy like a lighthouse's lantern, piercing the deep, dark fog of night.

BALLOON

ALEXANDER AWAKENS on the ceiling each morning, his face pocked and flecked with pieces of the popcorn surface. He has to push himself down to his empty bed. This is what happens when he dreams of her. His body fills with love, like a balloon filling with helium, and he rises, the covers unable to contain or restrain him. He floats until he is unable to go any higher, and like that balloon, he dances along the surface of the ceiling each night, not wanting to dream of her, but unable to stop, wandering hopelessly if she's doing the same.

THE BOY AND THE TREE

IN A SMALL ROOM sits a little boy. The little boy is staring at a television. On that television is another little boy who is staring at a tree.

Just outside that small room stands a tree. The mother of the little boy asks him, "Why are you sitting here looking at a little boy looking at a tree, when you can walk outside and look at a real, living tree yourself?"

The little boy does not hear her, though, because he's riveted by the television screen in front of him, where a little boy sits looking at a tree.

THE ART OF NOT WRITING

SHE CLAIMS she doesn't write the stories, that they write themselves, that winged muses descend from some ethereal plane to place their hands on the keyboard of her MacBook and type story after story, each one, like Athena, leaping from Zeus's head, fully formed in the battle gear of writers, coffee in hand, the editing happening somewhere in the heavens so once the story appears in this realm, it's perfect in a way that's not completely hers—if hers at all—and that the source of all this magic is not her simply sitting in her chair and just writing.

55

———

QUEENS

OR MEMORY OF A SUNSET

THEY STOOD on the rooftop of their apartment building, gazing at each other, the auburn sun descending across the horizon. The camera hung at his side, his eyes hungry from seeing her beauty through the curated lens of his Leica. He wanted to take in the moment, the sweet smells of summer dusk, the faint sounds of Corinne Bailey Rae crooning "Breathless" from a boombox down below, the feel of her brown skin glowing beneath his fingertips, the taste of her mint julep still lingering upon his lips. Years later, after they'd had three children, he'd return to that moment.

MUSICA

THE HORNS BLOW the chords of the arrangement and the drummer drops the beat like thunder clouds releasing rain on a drought, and the bass—oh the bass—it slithers between the percussion, like a serpent shedding syncopation. Her voice enters this milieu, thick, raspy with words that push the air in ways that cause our bodies to sway. The guitar strums like a Roberta Flack lyric, and we are mesmerized by the melody, like children unable to look away from a unicorn galloping across a playground. We take this in, our cells tingling in the resonance once it ends.

57

———

FINITY

SHE STARES INTO THE NIGHT, as if anticipating that a comet might streak the sky, always aware of the moon's phase. Some nights she can see only darkness above, the clouds seemingly erasing the universe's majesty in a single stroke. Other nights she can see nearly every constellation, the sky so clear it feels there is nothing separating her from space.

He sits next to her, holding her hand, wanting to say something so grand that it measures up to the miracles overhead, but he is left with English's twenty-six lowly letters, which can only be arranged in finite ways.

COTTON CANDY

SHE LOVED COTTON CANDY, the feel of the sugar tufts brushing against her skin, even the coarseness of the wet pieces that hardened into tiny bricks of sugar. The colors, pink and blue and yellow, all colors and flavors competing for attention on her palate, aroused more than her hunger.

She wondered what it would feel like to wear it, to sleep on it, to have it as hair she could style. She relished this idea until she realized that people would one day want to touch and pull and squeeze her cotton candy, and she could never allow that.

59

RAIN

She refuses to leave her home for fear that it might rain—frogs, locusts, impenetrable clouds of sand. Her existence is a literal one, and she has sheltered herself against the physicality of the words, building a home within the building that houses her. When it storms, she closes her eyes, hearing the heavy sounds pelting against the roof of her roof. She is afraid and wishes for those things to turn into water not deep enough to drown in. When she opens her eyes, the world is wet with water. This is her constant prayer, while she remains indoors.

ONLY MONSTERS HERE

HE HAS NO BUSINESS HERE. This is where souls come to die, our imaginations atrophied in the shadows of potential. We are the crumbs from our own meal, roaches are pets on invisible leashes, and we hunt at night, sweeping streets with eponymous tools. We are America's nightmare, the underbelly of the dream they tried to sell our parents.

He has no business here. The sun shines on him, his cells producing chlorophyll, that green that signifies health, prosperity, and security.

He's our savior, and we're united in keeping the light on those upon whom it was meant to shine.

61

—————

SIGNS

I STEPPED off the bus into a puddle of muddy water. It quickly seeped through the mesh of my running shoes, chilling my toes. I could hear the bus behind me slowly pulling off, its engine groaning like a dying apatosaur, water slapping against my calves, soaking my jeans. I started to jump to dry ground, but I realized that it didn't matter. What was done was done, something I couldn't outrun. Ahead of me a homeless man stood, holding a sign that read "You are now here!" He looked at me and gave me a nod. I nodded back.

THE POET

SHE WAS on a quest to write the perfect haiku. In elementary school, she'd learned the basics of the Japanese form (at least as represented in the West): five syllables, seven syllables, then a final five syllables, combined with some connection to nature. She had even gone on to learn that, in Japan, haiku are often written as a single line. She'd studied Bashō and Buson, as well as the wealth of Western poets who'd adopted the form. All to learn this tiny form.

But she knew the size belied its depth, the testament to what a poem could be.

BROOKLYN
OR HOTTER THAN JULY

CHILDREN DANCE IN THE STREETS, hydrant water gushing in arcs behind them, creating faint rainbows against the hot air of a summer day. Boomboxes play in front of brownstones, bringing Brooklyn alive with salsa, hip hop and reggae, cultural spices sprinkled throughout the streets.

Italian ices dissolve on dry tongues, leaving red and blue traces. Ronald kisses Tina to taste the difference in flavors, but it's all sugar, all sweet, like memories they will tuck into this soundtrack and store for later, when the summer ends, and think back to this moment, when the water sprinkled them like a shower.

VOCABLES

She speaks so softly that he must lean in closer to hear her, the slight puffs of air from her words tickling his ear, causing him to lift his shoulder to his ear, making it even more difficult to hear, and she smiles at what her words can do, and he smiles at her smiling at what her words can do, and with each exhalation of their joy, they are growing closer, dare I say "falling in love" with each other, as if life were intended for moments like this, where two people could converse without really understanding the other.

65

SNOW

THE SNOW, still fresh and untouched, stretches for miles across the plain, liquid-like beneath the swollen sun, and I think of her. In my memories she is dancing, calf-length boots nearly covered in powder. Her smile extends beyond the viewfinder of my camera and merges with the cobalt horizon, and love carries on the wind like an echo stretching itself across the vastness of some hidden canyon.

"Put the camera down," she says, reaching for me—but I don't, afraid that if I do not capture this moment, it might be lost to us forever, should our separate memories fail.

THE UNIVERSE IN HER PALMS

He watched her hand, delicate and soft, holding the pen gently in her loose grasp, and in that moment, he suddenly became aware of her: the radiance of her hair, the fullness of her lips, the way her nose wiggled almost imperceptibly when she smiled, the way her eyes danced as if everything that lay before them was somehow wondrous. How could he have overlooked all of this? It was as if her hands were the gateway to some previously hidden intoxicant. He longed to ask her name, to hold her hand, to simply be a satellite in her orbit.

THE DOOR TO ETERNITY

FOR HOURS, they drifted along on a cedar door, Teddy having convinced Allen it would be the perfect boat. Just the door and two branches they'd found along the shore to use as oars. No one knew they were out there.

The summer was hot and long, and the 80s were full of latchkey kids getting into all sorts of mischief before their parents got home. They were only supposed to go out a little ways, but the tide gradually changed their plans.

By moonlight, the wave looming over them was barely visible. Then water enveloped them, swallowing them whole.

A MOMENT IN MACY'S, CIRCA 1993

THE SONG quietly emerged from the staid Muzak-like tunes whispering from the speakers in the department store. She hadn't expected to move, to *dance*, but something in the groove caught her, pulling her away from the dress rack and out of her comfort zone. Closing her eyes, she committed to the music.

An amused retail associate quickly ran to the back to turn up the volume. A nearby child joined in, as did her father. Other customers began to dance, and one kid began doing *Fame*-like movements.

And no one pulled out a smartphone—because they hadn't been invented yet.

I NEED TWO PAIRS

I SPENT the summer cutting the yard, crushing the cans, picking up loose pecans from the backyard, washing dishes, and keeping my room clean to earn enough money to buy my dream kicks. At night, body aching, I envisioned what I'd wear with them, how I'd walk in them, where I'd go to be goggled by 'heads in the know.

I copped them right before school and made my grand entrance to oohs and ahhs.

But the months passed, and those same pristine grails wore down to beaters by year's end.

Next summer I'll have to save for two pairs.

A RECEIPT

SHE HELD his phone number for weeks, as if it were a receipt for an outfit she was unsure she'd return to the store—although she suspected she'd probably keep it.

But she understood nothing should come into your space until you are ready for it. Plus, he might be a *player*.

She hadn't offered him her number, but she'd accepted his. On a small slip of paper, like a store receipt.

It was possible he *was* genuine, authentic like a purse purchased directly from the store, but there was only one way to really know.

So she called him.

MANHATTAN

OR THE PERFORMANCE OF ART

HE LIKED to stand in front of the Basquiat, the bass of the boom bap in his Beats headphones vibrating, as if the paint on the canvas could somehow untangle itself and float into the air. *Picasso baby,* Jay Z had said, this intersectionality of life and art, this wild flame contained in a room where the kindling kept it ablaze for others to watch in amazement, wondering how art could detonate in one's soul.

As he gazed at it, he became the art.

He became Marina Abramović.

Then he became Marina Abramović looking at Jay Z looking at Basquiat.

AT NIGHT I TALK TO GHOSTS

My father once told me that dreams are a jambalaya of thoughts in your subconscious, tossed together, sometimes with a deft hand, sometimes with the skill of a first-year Russian circus bear, all for you to have small, intense experiences that you will likely forget before you awake.

Then I began to dream of *them*: deceased family and friends, walking about as if nothing had changed. I wanted so badly to tell them they were not alive, but I eventually sensed they understood this and were more interested in spending time with me and filling these voids in my heart.

THE LOVE POEM

THE POEM he wrote for her, she will never see, words written in the blackness of midnight, where echos of her body still tingle against his, these words, born of kisses long-since dried, evaporated sweat, dissipated passion, dropped onto the pages of a composition book like tears he promised himself he'd never shed.

Right now, he sees this poem as the best thing he's ever written, only because he has bound himself to a past that is no more, content to tease himself with romanticized ideas of what never was and what, if he were completely honest, never could've been.

BLACK CHARACTERS

THE ONLY THING more painful than dealing with the harsh realities of being Black in America is dealing with the harsh realities of being a Black character in a novel. I have picked more cotton, taken more lashes, and abused more loved ones than I'd care to remember. I have watched loved ones lynched—with rope or with government-issued ammunition—and seen myself blamed for all the ills of society. I have been the first one to die in a story and part of the community that needs saving by someone white.

Maybe it's not more painful—just the same.

THE GOAT

SHE SAW him sitting on a bench at the back of the park. He was leaning forward slightly, a kalimba resting in his hands. He plucked the tines, and she half-expected to hear him play one of his many hip hop hits. Instead, he played a pentatonic melody that was soothing and seemed to float on the breeze like a newborn butterfly. She wanted to walk over and ask for his autograph, but he seemed so *at peace*. Gone was his wild public persona, years in his rearview. He was still the GOAT, though, as he played softly to himself.

LINE BREAKS

WILL LINE breaks make this more of a poem, give the proper emphasis to each word, deepening its meaning? Maybe line breaks are like break beats—broken, but in a good way—those breakdowns in forgotten songs, the ones that bring the b-boys to the floor. These pieces, split apart from the whole to form a new, different kind of whole, making your head nod, juxtaposing the original and transcending it. These words snapping their fingers, making your eyes dance.

But, alas, this is not really a poem (or is it?), the line between fiction and poetry buried in ambiguity.

BRONX

HOME OF THE BOMBERS

MY GRANDFATHER still dons his pinstripe jersey on game day, the one with the 44 on back, and if you ask him about it, he'll tell you the story of what he was doing on October 18, 1977, when Reggie Jackson hit three consecutive home runs (on the first pitches from three different pitchers) in the sixth game against Los Angeles in the World Series.

Together, we watched Jeter's last game and hung a banner for number 2 in our memorabilia room.

Now we discuss Judge and what he will do for us, all while he wears his 44 jersey.

AKINETIC PROJECTILE

I AM the bullet that was never fired. I never had the opportunity to meet Henry Dumas, Trayvon Martin, John Crawford III, Michael Brown, Tamir Rice, Oscar Grant, Breonna Taylor, Daunte Wright, Medgar Evers, Martin Luther King Jr., Jamar Clark, William Chapman, Walter Scott, Eric Harris, Jerame Reid, Akai Gurney, Dontre Hamilton, Aiyana Jones, Amadou Diallo, Ahmaud Arbery, Jordan Davis, Emmett Till, and a multitude of others. As a result, they lived to ripe old ages without memories that I was ever near them. I did not alter their fates. I did not fracture their families. I was never there.

THE FAMILY OF HIS DREAMS

He does't know how the dreams began. In them, he sees himself thirty years into the future: a wife, a son, a granddaughter. In this future, his granddaughter develops leukemia, and his son turns to alcohol. His wife begins to struggle with depression, and he must use every ounce of himself to hold his family together.

In the present, though, he is a single man who works odd jobs and occasionally gets drunk on the weekends. He has no family to speak of, except for those in his dreams, the family his subconscious has conjured to give his life meaning.

THE GIRL AT THE PARTY

IT WAS an urban legend they'd handed down to freshmen for years, a rites of passage, where they told of a girl at a party, a beautiful soul who, incidentally, welcomed conversation from an awkward admirer. The two talked for hours, and he eventually offered her a ride back to her apartment. But just as they drove past a mysterious cemetery on the way home, she hopped out, never to be seen again. Later, the guy would learn that she'd died decades earlier and that he'd been talking to her ghost.

Every urban legend has to start somewhere, though. Right?

RUBY SNEAKERS

SHE LOVED HIM, and he loved her—so much that he supported her dreams to leave for Europe.

She wondered how he could let her go so easily, but she couldn't fathom what he wanted for her: something greater than himself, something that would fulfill and satiate her life.

What he didn't know is that she would have given up those treasures for the sensation of resting her head against his chest, as he whispered her name in his resonant baritone.

"Just click your heels three times and you'll come to me," he said.

She wanted desperately to believe him.

HE IS NOT HERE

Do not talk to him.

He is not here—nor has he ever been here.

What you are seeing is a figment of your imagination.

No, I don't see him either, but I know how you must feel.

Trust that your eyes have failed you, that your ears have failed you, that your sense of smell has failed, that your fingers have not touched anything but the idea of something your brain has created: an apparition, an idea.

He is not here. Do not talk to him.

We cannot make him something he is not.

We cannot make him real.

MELANIN

FOR MUCH OF HER LIFE, she denied its presence in her skin, as had her mother and her mother's mother. It was easier that way, navigating Southern cities, but it was always a dangerous proposition—the living in fear that someone would whisper a rumor (that was the truth) and the wondering if an ancestor's phenotypical traits might emerge in a newborn, her watching the ears carefully, praying they were not a shade too dark to tip the scale. The ironic part was as she watched The Culture blossom, she was relegated to the sidelines, her heart longing for more.

AFROFUTURA

YOUR LIPS ARE the dreamy synths of a 70's Stevie Wonder song. Your tongue sends me out into a galaxy contained within a single drop of dew, pooled along the vein of a leaf. You can tell me anything, and I will follow you. I breathe you like an intoxicant, your body pulling me toward the heavens, and there you electrify every cell of my being with your touch, ecstasy rolling in waves, crashing against moon rocks, beating our souls against these sinful shores.

But we are not making love on the ceiling.

The house is simply upside down.

SHIT DON'T CHANGE UNTIL YOU GET UP AND WASH YO ASS
FOR KUNG FU KENNY

HE IS NOT ready to get out of bed. He is too tired to move. He will lie there and ignore her calls for him to get up and take out the trash. She, too, is tired but life must go on, she says. This damn edible hasn't even kicked in yet, she says, and I have too many clothes to fold. At least he could be helpful, she adds. But he doesn't want to get out of bed. Sleep is sitting on his face. Frustrated, she rolls him up in his comforter, seals it, then takes a strong toke.

DOOKIE BLOSSOM GAIN, III FOR PRESIDENT

SHE VOTED ONCE FOR HIM—NOT that she would've voted twice (even though she really wanted him to win)—but she knew they might accuse her of shenanigans if he were to win, especially since he wasn't a politician—at least in the traditional sense—and had enemies from the womb, his Blackness sticking to everything he touched—be it words or woodwind instruments—and they didn't like that he told them the truth (to their faces, no less), didn't sugarcoat his words—splashing a "muthafucka" here and there—and she wanted her vote to count, so she voted once.

87 KEYS

THE LOW E flat on the old piano is dead. In his younger, more enthusiastic days, he used to play the piano hard, feverishly like a mad man on a trap set. Those were the days when he felt he'd live forever, that the music thundering through his soul sprang from an eternal well.

But then he snapped the string on the E flat, a loud gunshot pop that left gaps in his thinking. It was like trying to write without the letter "e."

He should've gotten it fixed, but he didn't, so now the piano sits there strangely silent.

WONDER WOMAN IN THE SWATS

Selene has wanted an invisible car since the moment she saw one on the TV show *Atlanta*. She is torn about whether to get the fully loaded luxury model or the factory standard version, though.

She has contemplated whether she should upgrade the stereo system, although she is unaware of any invisible systems.

She is also torn about whether she should spend the extra money for an electric edition.

She plans to drive it slowly so people can admire it.

She just needs to remember to park it away from all the other cars, so it doesn't get accidentally scuffed.

THE ART OF WRITING

THERE ARE millions of ways into a story, but I like going through the back window. I sneak in and catch the characters unaware, in flagrante delicto, their underwear bunched at their ankles. They need not tell me how they arrived at the dining room table. I can see that for myself and fill in the blanks without their assistance. I will write what is important in this moment, and once I am done, I will walk out the front door, leaving it wide open behind me.

I wonder how poets get into poems. Do they emerge from beneath them?

LOVE IS A LIE
OR SOME SHIT BASQUIAT WROTE

OSCAR HAS NEVER BEEN in love—or so he believes. How would he really know?

What is love? Is it great sex against a soundtrack of Maxwell and Sade, followup phone calls, picnics in the park, snuggling on the sofa watching a classic movie?

Is it attempts at being selfless, or buying flowers or diamonds?

Is it feeling quenched enough to not feel thirsty?

Maybe there is no love, only being in love with the idea of being in love.

But when she leaves, he feels the pain of her absence and begins to wonder if he's underestimated the possibilities.

HE WEARS THE MASK

THE CLOWN GOES to wash his face, but the makeup won't come off. No solution will work, and he slowly realizes that his clown face is now his everyday face.

At first people smile at him, occasionally waving at him. Still, no person can be happy all the time, and when his temper eases through the paint, he looks terrifying. He becomes the thing that people fear.

He cannot get a loan. He cannot find a lover. His employer fires him. He is alone.

No one can see his real self, the depth of his heart, hiding behind the makeup.

LAST NIGHT

THEO LIES IN THE DARKNESS, beneath the bedroom window of his apartment, gazing into the night sky through the haze of the city lights, Anita Baker's drowsy voice crooning about failed fairy tales in the background, and he is thinking about Alisha and last night—her last before returning to school—and how they made love beneath this very window, whispering their pleas for more time, promises destined by time and circumstance to fail, and there is an emptiness in the spot where she once lay, and, try as he may, he knows it will remain there until she returns.

93

—————

'TIL INFINITY

ON THE LAST day of school, they sat in the bleachers staring at the empty field. All of the days of eating lunch and cracking jokes, pulling off pranks in the hallway, fighting over who would step to Heather, trying not to think about this day, but it was now here. There was no more mischief left for them to get into. Graduation was days away, then some were off to college, while others were off to the military or looking for jobs. They vowed to keep in touch, to be boys forever, but they knew only time would tell.

OWNERSHIP

DEVONTE WILL USE his reparations check to buy an NFL team. He will scoop his talent from the combine, making sure to acquire those who jump the highest, run the fastest, and can lift the most weight. He will give them contracts that benefit himself more than the players. He will trade them during the middle of the season and put stress on their families, but he will dap each of his players beneath a banner of red, black, and green and talk about what they're doing for The Culture. He will call his team The Brothers—and mean it.

A HISTORY LESSON

DYLAN'S GRANDFATHER, even on his death bed, lamented the way his government had treated him after World War II.

"I come back to Jim Crow laws, can't do this, can't do that—and *I* fought for this country!—and they take that Nazi von Braun and give him an office and staff and the keys to the whole damn space program!"

Dylan wished the old man's dying words had been about love, hope, or forgiveness, but, as if pulled straight from Ralph Ellison's *Invisible Man*, he managed beneath labored breaths, "They write the history books, my boy. Just remember that."

THE COLLECTION

His walk-in closet looked like a Foot Locker stockroom. Boxes were stacked in columns brushing the ceiling, all of them empty, save the occasional unused extra laces he didn't want to lose, just in case he decided to sell them later. The sneakers themselves were stacked in clear plastic containers with hinged doors.

The reality is that he'd never be able to wear them all during his lifetime. Still, he liked the idea that he could, if he so chose to. They could've been unread books or Funko figurines. In the end, it was all about building a great collection.

MIRROR

THEY BOARDED A NEARLY EMPTY A train at the same time and, coincidentally, sat directly across from each other. Within a few seconds, they recognized their similarities: they were both wearing the same designer shirt, a high-end piece available only at the flagship store on Madison Avenue. One wore it unbuttoned and relaxed, while the other wore it completely buttoned up. Not only did their shirts match, but so did their skin tones and jawline beards. They even wore identical glass frames. On their feet, Jordan 1 Mochas, one tied, one loose.

Neither spoke, choosing instead to give the nod.

LIQUID PAGES

UNABLE TO CONTAIN HERSELF, she opened the book and dove into its pages, where she traveled to distant places in her imagination and had adventures that resulted in narrow escapes. Eventually, in the distance she would hear her mother calling her name, and like a person swimming upward from the bottom of a swimming pool, she would emerge onto the pages of the book just in time for dinner.

Each book on her bookshelf was like that, each one a different set of characters, a different setting, a different group of characters.

There was no substitute for a good book.

THE POINTER SISTERS

ANSON COULDN'T LET it slide: a writer making light of the Pointer Sisters, calling them occasional one-hit wonders. "Neutron Dance" was the focus of this particular literary ditty. That idea bothered him because, in *his* house, the Pointer Sisters were legendary and had numerous hits, his parents often singing their music to him. "Neutron Dance" and "Jump" were crossover hits. That's when it struck him that some white people view Black artists only by their most commercial songs. Anson shook his head. That writer would never really understand, so he vowed to write his own story about The Pointer Sisters.

LIFE IS A STAGE

HE SEES her on the R train (or maybe it's the W train), and he says hello. She responds in kind, and they start a conversation. She's studying nursing. He's a playwright.

No, he hasn't had a play produced. He's just full of potential right now—like her—but she's not interest in potential. She can do bad all by herself, she tells him.

What she doesn't know is that he is going to write a play one day where people will stand around waiting for Godot, who just so happens to be a bear that will chase them offstage.

ACKNOWLEDGMENTS

"Balloon" appeared in the *Hampton Renaissance;* "The Diver" appeared in *A Story in 100 Words; and* "The Novelist" appeared in *The Drabble.*

Thank you to Elle and Zoë for being my rocks.

Additional thanks to my family and friends who have supported me, as well as those readers who continue to enjoy my work. Thank you for helping me to live my dream.

ABOUT THE AUTHOR

Ran Walker (he/him) is the author of thirty books. His short stories, flash fiction, microfiction, and poetry have appeared in a variety of anthologies and journals. Prior to becoming a writer and educator, he worked in magazine publishing and practiced law in Mississippi.

He is the winner of the Indie Author Project's 2019 National Indie Author of the Year Award (selected by judges from *Library Journal, Publishers Weekly*, IngramSpark, St. Martin's Press, and *Writer's Digest*), the 2019 Black Caucus of the American Library Association Best Fiction Ebook Award, the 2018 Virginia Indie Author Project Award for Adult Fiction, and the 2021 Blind Corner Afrofuturism Microfiction Contest. Ran is an Assistant Professor of English and Creative Writing at Hampton University and teaches with Writer's Digest University. He lives in Virginia with his wife and much better half, Lauren, and his amazing daughter, Zoë.

ALSO BY RAN WALKER

B-Sides and Remixes

30 Love: A Novel

Mojo's Guitar: A Novel / (Il était une fois Morris Jones)

Afro Nerd in Love: A Novella

The Keys of My Soul: A Novel

The Race of Races: A Novel

The Illest: A Novella

Bessie, Bop, or Bach: Collected Stories

Four Floors (with Sabin Prentis)

Black Hand Side: Stories

White Pages: A Novel

She Lives in My Lap

Reverb

Work-In-Progress

Daykeeper

Most of My Heroes Don't Appear On No Stamps

Portable Black Magic: Tales of the Afro Strange

The Strange Museum: 50-Word Stories

Bees + Things + Flowers: Microfictions

The World Is Yours: Microfictions

Can I Kick It?: Sneaker Microfiction and Poetry

The Golden Book: A 50-Year Marriage Told In 50-Word Stories

Keep It 100: 100-Word Stories

A Burst of Gray: A Novel In 100-Word Stories

The Library of Afro Curiosities: 100-Word Stories

Black Marker: A Novel in 100-Word Stories

GloKat and the Art of Timing: A Novel in 100-Word Stories

A Different Kind of Christmas Story: A Carol in 100-Word Stories

Spaceships Don't Equipped With Rearview Mirrors: 50-Word Stories

This Is Not a Poem/Story: 100-Word Stories